BOYS RULE!

Skateboard Dudes

Felice Arena and Phil Kettle

illustrated by
David Cox

RISING ★ STARS

First published in Great Britain by
RISING STARS UK LTD 2004
76 Farnaby Road, Bromley, BR1 4BH

Reprinted 2004, 2005

For information visit our website at:
www.risingstars-uk.com

British Library Cataloguing in Publication Data

A CIP record for this book is available from the British Library.

ISBN: 1-904591-74-4

First published in 2003 by
MACMILLAN EDUCATION AUSTRALIA PTY LTD
627 Chapel Street, South Yarra, Australia 3141

Associated companies and representatives throughout the world.

Project Management by Limelight Press Pty Ltd
Cover and text design by Lore Foye
Illustrations by David Cox

Printed and bound in Great Britain by
Mackays of Chatham plc, Chatham, Kent

BOYS RULE!

Contents

Josh

Con

CHAPTER 1

Check This Out

On a quiet Sunday afternoon on the front steps of the local library, Josh is showing off his skateboarding tricks to his best friend Con.

Josh "Hey Con, check this out."

Josh squats down on his
skateboard with his hands almost
touching the ground. He suddenly
leaps up. He and the board are
airborne for several seconds. He lands
safely with both feet on the deck and
rides off without losing his balance.

Con "Wow, that's cool."

Josh "Yeah, it might look easy, but it takes a lot of practice. It's called an ollie."

Con "What about your pads and stuff—aren't you supposed to have them on?"

Josh "Ah, Mum says so but I don't need them."

Con "Can I have a go?"

Josh zooms off on his board
pretending not to hear Con.

Josh "Watch this!"

Josh rushes towards the steps that lead from the library's entrance. He shows no sign of slowing down. As he approaches the edge, he suddenly flings himself and the board over the steps and drops with a thud onto the pavement. He lands safely, again without losing balance.

Con "That was unreal! I never knew you were so good."

Josh jumps off his board and runs to the top of the steps. He slowly rolls around Con.

Josh "Thanks. That's called an acid drop. There are these steps near my auntie's place where I practise when I have to go there ... so I don't get bored."

Con "Give us a go now."

Josh "Hey, check this out."

Con is becoming more and more frustrated with Josh. He decides to run directly in front of Josh, making him stop abruptly only a few centimetres from him.

Con "I said, 'Can I have a go?'"

CHAPTER 2

Trick Lessons

The boys hang around, not making
eye contact. They continue to nag
each other.

Josh "No you can't."
Con "Why?"
Josh "Because."
Con "Because why?"

Josh "Because it's my board and I don't want you wrecking it."

Con "I won't wreck it. I just want a quick go."

Josh "You don't even know how to skateboard."

Con "Yes, I do."

Josh "Then how come you broke your arm on one when you were away last holidays?"

Con "That wasn't my fault. I didn't know there was a humungous hill coming up. It just got a bit fast, that's all. And now my folks have banned me from skateboarding for a whole month."

Josh "Yeah, right. Well how come you didn't tell me that before?"

Con "I don't know. I didn't think it was cool."

Josh "I think you're just saying that
   to make me feel sorry for you ... so
   I'll give you a go."
Con "Err ... no way. I don't want
   you feeling sorry for me. Forget it
   then."

Con turns and begins to walk
away from Josh.

Josh (shouting) "Hey! Where are you going?"

Con "Home."

Josh "Wait. You can have a go now."

Con stops and heads back to Josh.

Con "I can?"

Josh "Yeah, but let me just show you this."

Josh pushes away on his
skateboard and once again zooms
towards the edge of the steps. This
time, as he approaches the edge, he
flips his board onto a rail that runs
along the steps. Josh grinds his way
down the rail but suddenly loses
his balance towards the bottom. He
topples over and hits the ground
with a hard whack.

Josh (screaming) "Arrrwhhh! My ankle!"

CHAPTER 3

Take Two

Con rushes to Josh's side. He helps him up but Josh finds it painful to stand on his right foot.

Con "Are you okay?"
Josh "I can't believe I fell. I usually get that trick."

Con "It looked amazing until the very end. But are you okay?"

Josh "Yeah ... I think. I might've sprained my ankle."

Con "It looks swollen."

Josh "It really stings."

Con "Maybe you should get some ice on it or something."

Josh "Nah. I'll be okay. I'll just walk it off."

Josh attempts to walk but groans in pain as he steps down on the swollen foot.

Josh "Maybe you're right. I better go get it looked at. Mum'll freak— she told me not to skate without safety gear."

Con "Lean on me and I'll help you get home."

One week later Josh is back skateboarding again around the entrance of the local library. Con soon appears.

Con "Hey Josh. Haven't seen you all week. Looks like your ankle's better."

Josh "Yeah. It was only a small sprain."

Con "So, what about my go then?"

Josh "What?"

Con "You were going to give me a go on your board last week—just before you hurt yourself. Remember?"

Josh "Oh yeah. Um ..."

Con "Well?"

Josh quickly changes the subject, still not really wanting Con to ride his skateboard.

Josh "Do you want to come with me to watch a skateboard competition? It's on next Sunday. All these awesome skateboard champs are coming to town."

Con "You kidding? That would be *so* unreal."

Josh "Cool. Ask your folks and if it's okay, I'll meet you outside your house on Sunday at 10 o'clock. Right, here goes ..."

Con "Here goes what? And what about my go?"

Once again Josh ignores Con. He races off on his board and attempts the same trick that caused him to sprain his ankle only a week before.

Con "What are you doing? Are you crazy? You're goin' to hurt yourself again."

But it's too late. Josh jumps onto the rail and slides down the rail. Again, he falls off. This time he breaks his wrist.

CHAPTER 4

Skateboard Spectacle

It's the day of the skateboard championships. Josh (who now has his wrist in plaster) and Con are among a large crowd seated in front of a giant U-shaped ramp. They're watching a number of professional skateboarders show off their style.

Josh "That's so cool! That's what they call a drop in."

Con "They're really good."

Josh "Awwrh, what an awesome drop 180-degree kick turn!"

Con "How's your wrist?"

Josh "Okay. It comes with being a great skateboarder. I bet these guys have broken bones all the time."

Con "Yeah, but at least they're wearing the right protective gear. You really should wear your wrist guards and knee pads."

Josh "Yes *Mum* ... awwrh, unreal! Did you see that?"

Suddenly an announcement comes over the loudspeakers, calling for anyone in the crowd to have a try on the ramp. The crowd goes wild, especially Josh and Con.

Josh "No way! Why did I have to break my wrist! Awwh man, they would've picked me."

Con "Yeah, or me."

Josh "Err, in case you've forgotten, you're not allowed to skateboard."

Con "Yes I am."

Josh (scoffing) "Yeah right. What's with your story about being grounded for a month?"

Con "It's true! And by the way, my
month is up today. I'm not
grounded anymore. So I can
skateboard again."

Josh "Oh what! He's pointing at
you!"

Con "What?"

Con turns to see an official pointing directly at him, beckoning him to come out of the crowd and have a go on the U-ramp. Con excitedly accepts. Josh can't believe it.

Josh "Now look who's crazy! *You* can't skateboard."

CHAPTER 5

Finally My Go

Con is padded up by a couple of officials and is given a skateboard. He begins to roll up and down the ramp. He picks up speed, then all of a sudden is doing some amazing tricks, like a professional. He flips, kick-turns, twists and does an ollie grab. The crowd roar and cheer, and Josh watches, totally amazed by his friend.

Josh (to himself) "He really *can* skateboard."

Con "Yahoo!!!!!!!!"

Con finishes his breathtaking routine. He returns to Josh as the crowd claps, impressed by his terrific performance.

Con "So *now* do you think you'll be able to let me have a go on your board?"

Josh simply nods his head, speechless. And as for Con, he can't stop smiling for the rest of the day.

Josh

Con

Skateboard Lingo

deck The top surface of a skateboard.

nose grind When you grind on the front trucks of your board. Not when you pick your nose!

ollie When you and your skateboard leap into the air. This is the first trick that you learn on a skateboard.

trucks The trucks are the metal bars attached underneath the deck of the skateboard. The wheels are attached to the trucks.

BOYS RULE!

Skateboard Must-dos

☞ Make sure that you oil your trucks before you use your board.

☞ Cover your knees and elbows with padding. It really hurts if you fall on your knees or your elbows!

☞ Try to go as fast as you can. You might be able to set a new record for the fastest skateboard rider in the world.

☞ With the help of your friend, build your own skateboard ramp.

☞ Invent your own skateboard trick.

☞ If you are going to use materials from your father's workshop, make sure that you ask him first.

☞ Sometimes it is fun to get your sister to tow you around the park on your skateboard.

☞ If you want your skateboard to go faster, you have to either push harder or go down a big hill.

☞ The most important thing to remember is that you have to always wear safety gear when you ride a skateboard.

Skateboard Instant Info

- The first skateboards were more like scooters. They date back to the early 1900s.

- In the 1950s the trucks that are now on skateboards first became popular.

- In 1970 the first urethane wheels were made and used on skateboards. These are the wheels that are used today.

- Fifty million skateboards were sold in a three-year period from 1962.

Almost fifty per cent of skateboard injuries result from hitting uneven surfaces or surfaces with sticks, stones and cracks.

Over sixty per cent of injuries occur in the hands, arms and wrists.

Skateboards today have flexible decks and narrow wheels. These things make it easier to do tricks and to make them go faster, but modern boards are not as stable as the older-style skateboards.

BOYS RULE!

Think Tank

1 What is a skatepark?

2 What is an ollie?

3 How do you make your skateboard go faster?

4 Should you wear a helmet when you ride your skateboard?

5 What is a nose grind?

6 What is a flip?

7 What is a kick flip?

8 What is a board slide?

How did you score?

- If you got all 8 answers correct, then you should become a professional skateboarder.

- If you got 6 answers correct, make sure you don't move out of the park.

- If you got only 4 answers correct, then maybe you should keep practising or just ride your bike.

Felice → ← Phil

Hi Guys!

We have loads of fun reading and want you to, too. We both believe that being a good reader is really important and so cool.

Try out our suggestions to help you have fun as you read.

At school, why don't you use "Skateboard Dudes" as a play and you and your friends can be the actors. Set the scene for your play. What props do you need? You might like to bring your skateboard to school. You might like to try to make your own skateboard ramp.

So ... have you decided who is going to be Josh and who is going to be Con? Now, with your friends, read and act out our story in front of the class.